MAMMALS

MAMMALS

James Robert Herndon

OMNIDAWN PUBLISHING
RICHMOND, CALIFORNIA
2014

Cover art: "Panda Madness" by Hermawan Susanto, Cerah-Art

Cover design by Meg Alexander

Typefaces: Adobe Garamond Pro & Myriad Pro

Cataloging-in-Publication Data is available from the Library of Congress

Published by Omnidawn Publishing, Richmond, California
www.omnidawn.com (510) 237-5472 (800) 792-4957
10 9 8 7 6 5 4 3 2 1
ISBN: 978-1-890650-72-8

For Miranda

The first person to visit me in prison was a stranger, about fifty years old and clearly not even a distant relative. He sat with exceptional posture, one hand cupping the fist of the other hand in his lap. The part in his black hair exposed a sharp white line of scalp. The pocket inside his suit jacket was filled with unsalted pretzel nuggets, and throughout our conversation, he slowly removed one nugget at a time, lifting it to his mouth and rubbing it against his large lips before biting into it. When I entered the visiting room, hoping to see you, this is who I encountered.

Dr. Au-Yong—that was his name—stood up when I entered, and extended his arm toward me. I'd never shaken a hand before, and it felt wrongly intimate, a little invasive even, to be touched by someone I didn't know before anything else could happen. I noticed a starched white lab coat he'd folded neatly over a nearby chair.

"What do you know about *Ailuropoda melanoleuca?*" he asked.

No small talk about prison food or my dreams for the future. No effort made to act like a normal person and explain himself.

"I don't know what that is," I said.

"The giant panda, what do you know about it?"

"It eats and sleeps all day. People like to take pictures of it. It's a combination of raccoons and bears."

"It is a bear," he said, his voice suddenly deeper. "What do you know about mammals?"

"Are you a social worker?"

"What do you know about mammals?"

"They don't lay eggs."

He reached slowly into the pocket inside his jacket. "What else?"

"They stay with their families."

"Some of them, yes," he said, surprised. "Can mammals learn values?"

"Probably."

He smiled at me for the first time and pulled a contract out of his pocket. I needed you there, Dasu. I needed an older brother to smack my head, call me an idiot, and ignore me indefinitely. But yes and no were suddenly real options, and I said, "Yes, something new, please," when I had the right to say, "No, less newness, please." As if I could draw an open-ended life with my signature. If I had said no and refused to sign his contract, I'd still be at Tuen Mun Juvenile Detention Center in Hong Kong, serving out a ten-year sentence. With clean blankets and hot meals. Not an indefinite sentence. Out here.

The following morning, I was escorted out of Tuen Mun by an armed guard and driven to Lin Panda Breeding Center, where Dr. Au-Yong had prepared a cell for me—a white windowless room with a white wooden door instead of bars and no door handle on the inside. A small silver drain was installed in the middle of the tiled floor. A gray digital clock hung with cold self-possession from the wall over the toilet. A bed stood on tall aluminum insect legs in the opposite corner from the toilet. The bed springs were as thick as fingers, and every time I rolled over, I sounded like an 18-wheeler turning onto a hill.

The cell's only source of color sat next to my bed, on the floor. It was a round pink pillow, no bigger than a laptop computer. The pillow was much heavier than it looked, and there was an on-off switch on its side. It was a heating pad. In a darker shade of pink, a name had been sewn into it: Mei Li.

Dr. Au-Yong walked into my room at 5 a.m. the next morning, looking wide awake in a deliberate way. My white scrubs were itchy, but I'd kept them on and hadn't slept.

"Good morning, my young friend," he said. "Are you feeling prepared?"

I looked at the blindfold in his hand and didn't reply.

"Yes, that's for you. We have to take precautions. Please put it on."

Having signed the contract, I was legally obligated to participate in Dr. Au-Yong's program for the full duration. With some luck, I'd shorten my sentence. I was no fool, Dasu: I knew who had final say in the matter. At least he'd stopped pretending I had options.

"Are you ready to meet your roommate?"

He held my arm and walked me out of the room, down a long hall of echoes. I assumed it was a hall. My bare feet were scuffling quietly on what felt like linoleum, while Dr. Au-Yong's flat-bottomed dress shoes slapped the ground loudly, booming like fireworks over Kowloon Bay. He led me around several corners, his fist clenched tightly as if preparing... For what? What did he think the wayward *pok gai* he'd found in jail was capable of?

The temperature rose. An acrid, earthy smell. When Dr. Au-Yong took off my blindfold, I was in a gymnasium filled with warm bright lights. Aisles of particleboard tables were covered with nearly one hundred terrariums. When the creatures in the terrariums saw us, they began to claw the glass walls of their enclosures. They sounded like a rainstorm of toenails as we walked down the center aisle, almost all the way to the end. Dr. Au-Yong motioned for me to come closer.

Beneath the glare of a heat lamp was a flesh-colored rodent. It could barely move, save for the half-second lifts of its hairless head and the flexing of pink claws. Dr. Au-Yong leaned over and whispered something to the animal, and he turned to me like a host at a costume party. "Won, this is Mei Li. Clean your hands, lower them into the terrarium, and hold them in front of her."

There was a pump bottle of antiseptic lotion on the table. I pumped it four or five times, until Dr. Au-Yong nodded. He continued to nod as I covered my hands and forearms with the stuff. From somewhere deep inside me, you mimicked his nod and called him Captain Anus and *cat tau,* and I had to conceal a laugh.

"Do they ever attack humans?" I asked.

"Yes, if you do anything sudden or stupid. Hold your hands in front of her face and do not move them."

"Will my hands smell like meat to her?"

"Hold your hands in front of her face and do not move them."

I felt like I was lowering my hands into a garbage disposal. I clenched my muscles, waiting to be mauled, but my knuckles came to rest on a bed of short artificial grass at the bottom of the terrarium. Mei Li's head lifted and dropped a few more times, but it hung in the air slightly longer each time. The razor slits of her black nostrils fluttered in the stale air. She opened her coin-sized claws and brought them down on the plastic grass, clenching tightly. She began to move toward my hand like a dry snail, her spine rippling from tail to head as she drew herself forward. The first physical contact she made was with her tongue, on my right ring finger.

"Clutch her beneath the shoulders with both hands, and use your fingers to support her head."

Mei Li's fragility was so apparent it was almost offensive, and when I held her, I was pretty sure I was holding something that would wilt like a plant if exposed to direct sunlight. She was gross—the warm, dry feel of her thin skin, the way it stretched and contracted in my hands to protect the even more fragile things it encased. Mei Li was like a scrotum. My future depended on a scrotum.

"Don't let her down, Won."

For the first three weeks, Mei Li did very little other than sleep, curled in a ring on her heating pad. "Leave the pad on," Dr. Au-Yong had ordered. When she woke up, she would open her eyes slowly and close them again very tightly, as if trying to swallow them through her sockets. Her blinks grew less intense the longer she'd been awake—I doubted the white walls were helping—and once she'd collected herself, she would look for me. When she found me, she'd open her toothless mouth wide, which freaked me out until I realized she was asking for milk.

I had to feed her from a bottle by hand, Dasu. She didn't like to move any more than she had to—you can relate—but her paws were surprisingly nimble, even at ten days old. If I started to daydream while I was feeding her, even for a moment, she'd snatch the bottle away from me. In order to get it back, I had to tickle each of her small paws until she released the bottle and latched onto my fist instead. After a few days, my hands were speckled with tiny red scabs, and I avoided thoughts of what they'd look like in twenty weeks. Every other day, Dr. Au-Yong brought me warm rags and rubbing alcohol to clean myself with, along with a clean pair of scrubs and bedsheets. I'd hide my deteriorating hands behind my back as he set everything down on the floor, and checked the battery in Mei Li's pad like a doctor checking a patient's heart.

The pain Mei Li could inflict forced me to pay constant attention to her. She didn't look like a rat anymore. She looked like a bouncer the size of a toothpaste tube, stocky and tough, front paws facing each other; or a flat-faced albino bulldog, mostly naked, with a cobweb of white fur around her midsection. The exposed skin on her forearms was turning from pink to black; so was the skin around her ears and eyes. Her hair would be black on those spots, and white on the rest of her. I'd only seen pandas on television, and it felt odd to see one like this. It was as if nature had started to create a panda, then got sidetracked and forgot to finish.

Mei Li couldn't hold eye contact very well, but I tried to encourage it. Maybe because I was looking at her so much and I wanted to even things out. Before you were embarrassed to be seen with me, we tried to get that guy in the office building to look at us. Remember? We were clawing at his window, and you pressed your butt up against the glass, and I screamed like a hawk, and after a while we finally said, "What is wrong with this guy?" and walked away. That's how I felt around Mei Li, even though I knew better. I knew she was too young to think about what she was seeing, and I knew she wouldn't think about it very much even when she got older. I still put myself in her field of vision.

Dr. Au-Yong brought us food every night: soggy lo mein for me, a bottle of warm milk for Mei Li. "You are wondering what I expect of you in my program," he said one evening.

"You haven't told me how to teach Mei Li anything."

"Trust your intuition, Won. How you teach Mei Li good behavior is, I'm pleased to report, entirely up to you. That is *your* test. I need to see how thoughtful you can be, how much creativity you are willing to bring to your teaching. Your commitment to Mei Li will show how committed you are to changing your own ways."

"I don't understand."

He laughed politely. "I have faith in you, Won. Promise me you will do your very best. Remember, you only get three tests, and your first test is in three weeks. If you feel anxious or uncertain about how things are going, you must try something else immediately. A man of success is always sure of himself."

"I'll be pardoned if I pass all three tests?"

"Good luck, Won."

Three weeks later, I found a note on the food tray.

Won,

Please feed Mei Li at 4 a.m. tomorrow morning. At 5 a.m., you will show me that you can facilitate excretion.

Warm regards,

Dr. Au-Yong

Mei Li was too young to "facilitate excretion" herself. I fed her beforehand like Dr. Au-Yong told me, and she didn't try to steal the bottle. But when Dr. Au-Yong came in at 5 a.m., she refused to leave her heating pad. I had to pry her off using the only technique I'd discovered: tickle each paw until it attacked the tickling hand. The process took a humiliatingly long time. I waited for Dr. Au-Yong to say something, but he just sat there like a security camera at the edge of my bed, faithfully recording each laceration on his clipboard. When I finally pried her loose, I carried her to the center of the room and put her down on her back, next to the toolkit I'd been given. How getting a panda to shit demonstrated my commitment to good behavior was lost on me.

Inside the toolkit was a jar of artificial saliva and a long rubber tongue with an ergonomic handle at its base. I picked up the tongue and ladeled a generous helping from the jar. Mei Li had a light spasm as I slathered her neck and ran the tongue down the length of her newly furry torso and belly. Her limbs trembled involuntarily, and she opened and closed her mouth, chewing on the tense air. "Over and over in the same direction, slow gentle strokes, one hour after feeding." This had been scrawled on a note I'd found inside the toolkit, and I obeyed.

Minutes passed in silence. Dr. Au-Yong was watching, recording everything, but I just couldn't help it. When Mei Li relaxed, my mind was finally free to wander. I thought of Auntie Hui, our caretaker at the group home, and how she had to help the younger kids use the bathroom. Maybe—I don't know how this idea got in my head—this toolkit would've made life easier for her. A kid could jump in her lap and shout, "I'm ready!" and she could dip a giant tongue in homemade saliva and lovingly stroke the child until he peed himself. I thought I was laughing on the inside until I noticed Dr. Au-Yong frowning at me. Mei Li had a turd hanging halfway out of her butt. Embarrassed, I ran the tongue over her with quick brushes until she'd finished, and I could scoop the turd into a Ziploc bag.

When it was over, Dr. Au-Yong smiled with vague intent, like a baby with gas. I don't think he was impressed at all. But as he exited my room silently, he nodded.

I had passed.

The digital wall clock in my cell persisted, but Mei Li became the real clock. I woke up when she woke up. I ate after I fed her. I tried to sleep when she slept. If I couldn't sleep, I'd watch her sleep and feel the seconds tick by.

A few days after our first test, Mei Li woke up from a particularly long nap, and she made a noise.

"CHIPE!"

Dr. Au-Yong said that pandas aren't supposed to make noise.

"CHIPE!"

"Way to be! You show them! Great stuff!" Treating Mei Li like a young athlete felt stupid. But the ideal zoo animal is probably social, right? At the time, I thought Mei Li would live in a zoo someday, and so she needed to be interested in other animals, and I was trying to lead by example.

"CHIPE! CHIPE!"

"You are friendly! You can live in cramped quarters with other animals!"

"CHIPE!"

To cross the language divide, we'd need games, like the kind they made kids play. Games that rewarded politeness. These games were still inside me somewhere but I couldn't think of how they went, so I had to make up new ones.

When Mei Li was resting on her heating pad, I would twirl it like a merry-go-round. Or I'd rotate the pad so that her head faced the opposite direction from me, and I would drum on the bed or the floor drain and whistle "Seven Nation Army" until she had finished turning around to face me.

You and I had played games together, Dasu, but we never acknowledged it. Sidewalk Patrol, that was a good game. We never did anything horrible. We just wandered the neighborhood together and made fun of older men, the ones who wore suits and walked in perfect lines down the sidewalk like every day was a sobriety test, men who mortified us. Men like Mr. Feng.

Remember the day you had "stuff you needed to take care of," so you couldn't come to the Clint Eastwood store with me? "What kind of stuff?" I asked. You shook your head. I wanted to kick you, but I had secrets too, so I nodded and went to steal Xbox games by myself. You weren't there to block the owner's view while I made my grabs, but I was a fast runner like you. I bolted out the door and sprinted down the crowded sidewalk toward Mr. Feng. Everyone else saw me running like a lunatic and got out of my way. "Move!" I shouted at him, but Mr. Feng didn't move, and when we collided I checked him with my shoulder. He hammered the tip of the fire hydrant with the back of his head. A clink like a heavy stick striking a muted bell. His tongue stuck out of his mouth. It was punctured by his teeth. I ran. Other people stopped to see if he was okay, and they only saw the bite marks. Blood flooded his brain. I ran past the group home, past all our friends' homes. I tried to exhaust myself completely. It never occurred to me to hide.

〰️

When the second test arrived, Mei Li had reached the size of a wine bottle, and she had grown a delicate coat of black and white fur. Yes, of course I was nervous. You would have been, too; at least I'd never lie about it. I knew I was either on my way to seeing you soon, to play the stupid games I wanted to play, or I was on my way back to Tuen Mun. Based on the note Dr. Au-Yong slipped under my door the day before, these stakes excited him.

Won,

5 a.m. tomorrow = Test 2!

☺

"How does she respond to you, Won?" He came in at 5 a.m. and started talking before he'd made any eye contact. I hadn't slept. "Have you provided her with enough incentive to respond to you visibly? I'm sure you have."

I put Mei Li on her back in the center of the room and sat on the ground beside her. I had to let her stay on the heating pad this time—Dr. Au-Yong said she had to leave the pad by choice.

"Summon her."

I made a move to turn off her heating pad—incentive—and he barked at me.

"No cheating! She must come to you because other animals matter to her, not because she's desperate for heat."

The starch in my scrubs made me itchy, especially when I sweated. Squirming as invisibly as possible, I tried the usual tricks. I drummed on the tile. I whistled "Seven Nation Army" at her. I tried to make eye contact. She looked asleep.

"She's asleep, Dr. Au-Yong."

"She is not asleep."

The bottle: Mei Li didn't have it. I picked it up, aimed the nipple at her face, and waved it around the heating pad like a satellite.

"Bottle to Mei Li, bottle to Mei Li, can you hear me?"

She remained on her back, following my sad orbit without getting up, rolling from side to side in the direction closest to my offering, snaking her spine languidly, and digging herself deeper into the heating pad. I had trained her to trust that I'd meet her needs, whether she humored me or not. With positive attention guaranteed, she was doing what you would do: exactly what she wanted.

"Won…"

"Please wait."

"How often does she leave the heating pad?"

"She leaves it when I facilitate excretion and when I pull her off. She shows interest when I make eye contact, too."

Dr. Au-Yong shook his head, disappointed. "Your intuition is failing you, Won. It is essential that Mei Li be domestic, but not too domestic. You are turning her toward the latter."

I held up my scabby fists. "Do domestic pandas do this?"

"Yes. So do kittens. Listen to me: it is inevitable that Mei Li will crave a heat source. Do you understand? Captive pandas need a plentiful supply of body heat. No one knows why. Dorsal fins on captive whales go limp, yet the whales are perfectly healthy. You can't let these mysteries make you complacent, Won. I'm counting on you to do a better job of keeping Mei Li active, physically and mentally. She can have her heat source, but she mustn't be so dependent on it. A dependent animal is a helpless animal."

"Did I pass?"

"You have work to do."

And that was that: he stopped speaking to me.

He dropped off food and clean linens, picked up plates and dirty linens, dropped off empty shit bags and picked up warm shit bags. He gave Mei Li a rubber pineapple chew toy and cooed like a pigeon when he gave it to her. He ignored me completely. It didn't matter if I acted friendly or domestic or feral or stupid. I was given no attention, not even eye contact. Perhaps it was all part of the program; it was more or less official.

The silent treatment remained in effect until Test 3.

I wish I could tell you that things got better, Dasu. More honestly, I wish I could tell you exactly what you want to hear, and have it be the truth. What do you want to happen?

A. Things get worse for your little brother before they get better. (You want to believe me.)

B. Your little brother gives up, eats the failure, and goes back to Tuen Mun where he belongs. (You are rolling your eyes at me.)

C. Your little brother kicks Dr. Au-Yong in the balls, does a flip over Lin's perimeter fence, and rides back to

Hong Kong on Mei Li's back. (You are laughing *with* me.)

You can say, "All of the above," and I'll break my own ribs to make it true. I will always hate you for earning what you haven't earned from me. I will never let you out of my heart, and I will hate you as long as I live. I don't know how to teach Mei Li about this.

Here's what happened. I tried to be cocky because it was a rewarding habit, but the more I thought about my situation, how everything was out of my control no matter how much control I appeared to have, the more my nerves began to fray. Without meaning to, I'd make a noise in the back of my throat like a vibrating cell phone, then catch myself doing it and stop until I'd forgotten about it, then start again. The noise made Mei Li shifty and restless on the pad, as if she'd been cornered by poachers. When Mei Li got nervous, I got more nervous, so I'd repress my noise—then I'd resent her for forcing me to behave a certain way, and I'd stare angrily at her until she saw me staring. She'd get anxious, I'd get anxious, and so on. Maybe you enjoy being a role model. To communicate my frustration to Mei Li, I would yell her word whenever she did, with more volume and bile.

"How's the milk?"

"CHIPE!"

"CHIPE!"

She'd look at me with what appeared to be genuine bewilderment. But she could lie down on her heating pad and, so it seemed, forget the whole thing ten seconds later. My jealousy embarrassed me.

It got to a point where Mei Li and I barely interacted, and our training came to a halt. I'd kick the bottle to her from across the room. I let her shit and piss whenever she pleased. We played no games. I wasn't mad at her; I just needed a break from caring. Plus, despite what Dr. Au-Yong would have said, Mei Li was doing just fine on her own. Not only was she pissing and shitting freely without help, she was blabbing like an extrovert and doing laps around the room like she owned it, which she did. She had even taught herself how to climb; she could scale the toilet and the bed. She would wake me up on purpose. One night, I had a dream that we were back at the group home, but you were missing, and so I told Auntie Hui that I hadn't seen you in a long time. I was terrified that something had happened to you. But you were fine: you had been out with your older friends, which Auntie Hui had forbidden you to do, so you had to do all the bathroom cleaning for a month. Instead of punching me for being a tattletale like you would have done in real life, you sat on my chest. I was choking, and you said it served me right. I woke up gasping for air and discovered a hairy black-and-white animal curled up on my ribcage: Mei Li, bed climber, heavy as a cinder block.

Another night, the noodles Dr. Au-Yong delivered were so bad they turned to a salty mush on my tongue when I closed my mouth. They'd been made, I estimated, several days prior and had been left soaking in a high-tech rice cooker ever since. Auntie Hui had used two timers when she made lo mein: one for the noodles, one for the vegetables. I could taste her precision whenever I had some, the taut noodles easily coming apart in my teeth, evenly saturated with the homemade broth she'd boiled them in. On your birthday she made lo mein and rice pudding for us, a rare treat, and we stuffed our faces like we hadn't eaten in days. You remember. Even with as little as I eat here, I can still summon the feeling of being full on Auntie Hui's lo mein. The way the muscles in my abdomen would let go, forcing me to slouch or lean back in my chair; the wonderful sleepiness that washed over me; the saliva still pooling in my mouth, ready for more, though my belly had no more room. On your birthday, I'd stuck a wet lo mein noodle to my upper lip and curled the ends to form a thin mustache. I had nodded reverently in your direction, and said, "I think someone has a career in business ahead of him." I was pretending to be Mr. Lao, our group home's biggest donor. Mr. Lao wasn't a stuck-up *cat tau*, just an old-fashioned geek with a funny voice. An easy, almost lazy target for ridicule.

You knew who I was being, and you cracked up really hard. You pulled a noodle out of your own bowl and stuck it to your lip. "A first-rate observation, young man," you said in Mr. Lao's honky baritone. "Let's make plans for our prosperous future together!"

"Stop that," Auntie Hui had cut us off. "Mr. Lao deserves your respect." She glared at us, but we didn't stop.

"Very good, indeed," I said.

"Yes, yes," you said, nodding at Auntie Hui. Her face twitched slightly, and it seemed to bend in on itself.

"Enough. Stop, now."

We didn't stop. We kept pushing and pushing, you and me.

I remembered that day as I turned off Mei Li's heating pad.

She was quiet at first. Passing seconds ticked on, inaudible. Ten. Twenty. Thirty seconds: she stood up, stepped off her cold pad, and slowly came to me. I moved away. She crawled to me and I moved away, prolonging the feeling. I did it. Minutes ticked by.

Ten.

Twenty.

Thirty.

I did it until Mei Li gave up, and she collapsed with a violent plop on the tiles. Legs crumpled beneath her, face pressed against an invisible wall. She opened and closed her jaw very quickly four or five times, paused, waited for me, started over. Her in-breaths grew thick and moist, as if she were drawing air through a straw. The breathing of someone with the flu who has fallen asleep. Her soft whine turned into a soft whistle, a toy train whistle, getting louder. As the whistle grew louder it sounded less and less plastic. Her body used all its energy to turn itself into a noisemaker, hardening as her mouth opened wider. I could see the back of her throat, the raw wet flap. Purple veins in the flap. Louder. The volume stung my ribcage, was designed to sting my ribcage. The volume peaked, then fell slowly.

She was quiet. The longer I waited, the easier the waiting became. This had never happened to me before. I lowered my face to hers and made her stare at me. She stared back.

Black marbles coated in Vaseline: that's what her eyes had always looked like. At that moment, they looked like something that grew beneath a lily pad. I needed a word like she had. One single word that I could belt out over and over and feel articulate.

Mei Li had a gentle spasm when I clutched her beneath the shoulders. She pushed her body downward, into my palms, and her claws tightened their clench. I managed to extract my hands long enough to take my shirt off and drape

28

it over her. The blankets on my bed were a joke, no match for Lin's air-conditioning system, but I pulled every last one of them off the mattress and threw them over her. Not knowing if the blankets were thick enough to suffocate her, I sat under them too, using my seated body as a tent pole, and I kicked at the sides every minute or two, to let fresh air in. She wouldn't have suffocated. The skeletal blankets allowed enough light through the tent's walls to make her visible. She was silent, breathing gently again.

When she was warm enough to lift her head to look at me, I picked her up and placed her in the opposite corner of the tent. She crawled to me, sharp shoulder blades pressing almost out of her skin as they rotated, head and muzzle rolling from side to side as if she were sweeping the air clean, long claws clicking against porcelain tiles. She crawled so slowly that at times it seemed as if she were moving in place. She crawled to her mother.

<hr/>

Dr. Au-Yong slipped a note under the door the following morning.

Won,

Test 3 will take place at 7 a.m. today. Yes, later than usual, but daylight will be essential.

Warm regards,

Dr. Au-Yong

Mei Li was already awake, pulling apart the rubber pineapple Dr. Au-Yong had given her. I wondered if giving her the toy had been a trick of his, to see if she was capable of destroying something—because of course it would be my fault if she was. Bears are peaceful until they hang out with human teenagers. You can look it up.

"It's time to help each other, Mei Li."

She stopped mauling the pineapple every ten seconds or so as if she were perplexed by what she'd just done. When urge overwhelmed curiosity, she'd maul it some more. Mei Li was still little at twenty weeks, no bigger than a picnic basket. But she'd begun to resemble a tiny adult panda, and she weighed at least fifty pounds. There was thick white fur all over her wide forehead and short muzzle, and thick black fur around her ears and eyes. Her claws were two inches long, strong and sharp enough to rip a tree apart. It had been weeks since I'd let Mei Li claw my hands, and they still looked as if I had washed them with a cheese grater.

"You're going to do great today, you know that?" My stomach began to fold. "I need you to give me the pineapple, so you can do better than great. I'm going to hide it."

"CHIPE!"

"You can give me the pineapple, or I can take it from you."

When you held on to all the money we made selling Xbox games at school, do you remember asking me if it was okay?

"Fine."

I smacked the toy out of her mouth.

A dark red stain spread across my white scrubs. Getting bigger. Mei Li had smacked me back, so fast that I was already bleeding when I saw her do it. I yanked the pillowcase off my bed pillow and tore the flimsy white cloth into uneven strips as fast as I could. If Dr. Au-Yong saw what I'd made Mei Li do, I'd be in the next car to Tuen Mun. It was a sorry bandage, but I tied it around my midsection without looking down, not wanting to know how deep the cut was, and I pulled the bandage as tight as I could. Slow waves of nausea rolled upward from my abdomen to my head.

"*CHIPE! CHIPE!*" Mei Li's yaps were even sharper than usual. The white walls began to spin slightly, and the silver drain on the floor seemed to orbit my body.

"*CHIPE! CHIPE-CHIPE!*"

She stood on her hind legs, reaching her full modest height of two feet, and bared her teeth at me. Her jaws opened and closed. I wanted to hug her; I wanted to skin her. Wisely, I took a deep breath instead, knowing how easily she detected panic; perhaps I'd already infected her.

Dr. Au-Yong knocked on our door as he opened it. I crossed my arms over my belly, covering the wound. He ignored me and walked directly to Mei Li, beaming at her like an expert artist appraising his newest work.

"Hello, my precious girl," he said softly. "Are you ready to play?"

"CHIPE!"

The grin vanished from his face.

"That means different things at different times," I told him. "But I think it's mostly her way of saying, 'I am alive, I am here, and I am ready for your attention.'"

He looked at me as if I had just farted. "You, Won, are forbidden to talk from this point onward. We must evaluate how Mei Li behaves when she can't hear your voice."

Mei Li followed me into the hall. This was the first time I'd stepped outside my room in twenty weeks, and this time, Dr. Au-Yong hadn't blindfolded me. The walls were a dull, sickly white, and blemishes had been covered with tiny squares of white wallpaper. There was a short, scuffed green carpet, like the grass in a shopping mall garden, cold to the touch. A warm chime sounded. I held my arms tighter

32

across my body and hoped the bleeding had stopped. In the hallway, we passed many doors, and if things had worked out differently, I would have found out what was behind every one of them. I would have made it my mission to find out, and I would share every detail with you. We reached a wide, glossy black door at the end of the hall.

"Mei Li will walk from here to the testing center by herself. You will follow me."

He entered a code into a small keypad. Another warm chime sounded, and the mechanical door slid open like a stage curtain. A short dirt walkway led to a testing center at the forest's edge: an ashy sandbox, about the size of a McDonald's playground, surrounded by a chain-link fence. Inside the sandbox, three things formed a triangle: a huddle of shredded black tire swings; a slide made of thick blue plastic; and a silver tetherball pole, with a white tetherball at the end of a white rope. Fifteen panda cubs, the other test subjects, were going lazily wild. Two cubs had climbed onto the tire swings, and they lay on their bellies inside their tires, letting their limbs dangle in the warm air. In the open part of the sandbox, four cubs took turns wrestling in slow motion while another cub, a spectator, fought an invisible opponent, timing his movements with those of the visible wrestlers. Three cubs had figured out how to climb the blue plastic slide, and they drifted down the chute at the slowest possible speed. The remaining cubs, reluctant but still social, were sleeping in a pile next to the testing center's entrance.

I didn't have to guide or encourage Mei Li. She sauntered down the path and headed straight for the tetherball to play by herself. The rope was long enough for the ball to touch the ground, and upon reaching it, she clutched it with her foreclaws and began gnawing on it. My abdomen was scalding hot. There were coals inside it, and I turned away to spit. Dr. Au-Yong made a note on his clipboard. He signaled wordlessly to me, and I followed him to a viewing area by the playground's outer fence. I tripped while looking down at myself but I got up quickly. I was leaking. My bandage had soaked through, and it was getting harder to keep the dark spot covered. Dr. Au-Yong took rapid, illegible notes— I tried to read them—while I stared pensively at the testing area. Mei Li had approached the cubs at the slide to make friends. She dug a hole in the dirt at the bottom of the slide, and she lay on her back in it, her limbs splayed out in a shaggy X. Other cubs were drifting leisurely down the slide, and when they reached the bottom, they landed on her belly. She would swat lazily at them, not seeming to mind but going through the motions as if she did. After being landed on four or five more times, she rolled out of her hole and let a larger cub take her place there. She then followed the cub that had just landed on her to the steps of the slide, cutting it in line at the last moment before deftly climbing—I was actually proud—the steps to the top.

"CHIPE!" she said. The cub behind her on the ladder nudged her forward, sending her down the blue plastic chute at a fast clip. She landed on the large cub spread eagle in the hole, and instead of climbing over it, she nuzzled it.

She saw me. She was still on top of the other cub when she stood up and craned her head to look for me, to see me watching her. We made eye contact, and she held it! I gave her a thumbs up.

"RYACK!"

The panda in the hole shrieked. Mei Li ignored its aggressive swats and continued to nuzzle.

"RYACK! RYACK-RYACK!"

"Leave it alone, Mei Li!"

Dr. Au-Yong grabbed my arm. "Silence, please," he said.

Mei Li was looking for me again when the other panda clamped its teeth onto her ear, and whipped its neck from side to side as if prying a branch off a tree. There was a horrible rip, and my eardrums were split by a scream that I was unwilling to ignore.

Dr. Au-Yong didn't try to stop me when I hopped the fence. When I pulled Mei Li away from the psychotic cub, she was as heavy as a sandbag, but with a grunt and a flex, I was able to hoist her onto my shoulders, the wound in my side throbbing with its own pulse.

I kicked the other cub in the head as hard as I could. Something popped inside my bare foot, as if I'd kicked a rock wrapped in a towel.

I tightened my grip on Mei Li and hobbled to the far side of the sandbox fence, where the forest began. Lifting my good foot into the weave of the chain-link fence, I stood up and grabbed the top of the fence with one hand and pulled Mei Li off my shoulders with the other. She'd been terrorized, and she dug in her claws, tearing through my scrubs and lacerating the skin beneath. I screamed. I had to throw her over. My legs were trembling and my stomach had a hole, but I forced myself to move because I would know soon what you and I would do to celebrate our reunion, what I would say to you when I burst through your door with a wild animal at my side, how I would persuade Dr. Au-Yong to pardon me and to release Mei Li into my care, how I would seal the new holes in my body for good. A thin metal wedge on the top of the fence punctured the soft center of my good foot just before I fell to the other side. I hoisted Mei Li onto my shoulders and started to run.

James Robert Herndon lives in Atlanta, Georgia. He is a graduate of the Warren Wilson MFA Program for Writers and the Clarion West Writers Workshop. His fiction has appeared in *Halfway Down the Stairs,* and is forthcoming in an anthology of stories by Clarion West graduates. When not writing, he enjoys woodworking and being outside with his wife. His website is www.jamesrobertherndon.com.